Coming Home

THE SEQUEL TO *FLOWERS IN DECEMBER*

Books by Jane Suen

Children of the Future

FLOWERS SERIES
Flowers in December
Coming Home

ALTERATIONS TRILOGY
Alterations
Game Changer
Primal Will

SHORT STORIES
Beginnings and Endings: A Selection of Short Stories

Coming Home

THE SEQUEL TO *FLOWERS IN DECEMBER*

JANE SUEN

COMING HOME: The Sequel to *Flowers in December*

Jane Suen books are available for order through Ingram Press Catalogues

www.janesuen.com

Printed in the United States of America

First Printing: February 2019

Library of Congress Control Number: 2019901264

Paperback ISBN: 978-1-7323873-8-6
Audiobook ISBN: 978-1-951002-03-9
Ebook ISBN: 978-1-7323873-7-9

For my loved ones—two-legged and four-legged.

Here, now, and always.

Chapter 1

December 24

TWENTY-FOUR INCHES. The width of a countertop. Mary Ann stared at Connor across the space. It seemed farther, the distance between them. She pressed against the rigid surface of the counter, a reminder that something separated them. The noise and bustle in the flower shop had diminished, the crowd thinning as they made the last purchases before the store closed for Christmas Eve. Norma's chirpy voice floated in the air, as she cheerfully rang up sales for the old woman.

The white lights twinkled and danced. The light scent of flowers perfumed the air. Left alone at the counter with Connor, Mary Ann couldn't find her voice. Not the one she reserved for customers or the one she had used with Connor when he was more than just a customer and became something else—(or so it had seemed). When Connor left town four months ago, that voice became faint and distant, until something stilled it. It was replaced with questions, laced with uncertainty. She wondered why he hadn't called or contacted her.

Behind the facade of her pleasant smile, a lump caught in her throat. She clutched her hands behind the counter, keeping a grip on her emotions, holding back the anger.

It seemed like an eternity, but probably only a few seconds passed.

There was an awkward silence.

"How've you been?" asked Connor, his voice betraying a hint of anxiety beneath the surface.

Mary Ann nodded. She wanted to give him a piece of her mind. *Why did he wait so long to come back?*

"Your place is lovely—so festive," said Connor. He turned to look around the shop. Seeing the old woman departing, he gave her a smile—the one who had given Mary Ann and Connor a wink, as if she knew.

"It's my dream come true—my own flower shop," said Mary Ann. "I want to cater to every celebration—birth, love, marriage, anniversaries and holidays. For someone in the first bloom of love, the hopeful romantic, those wanting to make affirmations long after the wedding vows. The beginnings of life, the joys, hardships and illnesses that come after, and finally the end."

"You're passionate … and you've done a great job with it."

"Norma was a blessing. I couldn't have done it without her." Mary Ann gestured to her assistant, behind the cash register, grateful to have something to do with her hands, and for the chit-chat.

"Was this your idea? The holiday decorations?"

"My creative side took over."

"Weren't you an art minor in college?"

"You remembered ..." said Mary Ann, surprised he brought up a remark she had made, months ago.

Connor smiled. "So I did." He often admitted to himself how many times he replayed their conversation that night at Manini's restaurant—the things she had shared about her life; her story. He felt relaxed and comfortable with Mary Ann, and they talked easily then, as if they've been friends for a long time. No cautionary bells had rung.

"Mary Ann," said Norma, interrupting. "Would you like me to stay and close up?" Norma's voice was cheerful. Mary Ann looked at her assistant. She was tall and slightly plump, with a touch of matronly grace. Her hair was cut short and streaked with gray. She had a way with customers. No matter what the customer said, she remained calm, courteous, and business-like—at times effortlessly easing into the roles of a best friend, a confidante, a psychologist, a fortune teller, or whatever fit the situation at hand.

A quick glance confirmed the last customers were gone. It was a few minutes after closing time. "No, it won't be necessary," said Mary Ann. She reached under the counter and pulled open a drawer, taking out a box tied with a beautiful bow and a spray of rosemary tucked in it. "Merry Christmas, Norma."

"Oh, thank you," said a delighted Norma. "I'll put it under the tree and open it on Christmas Day." She set it carefully on the counter. Zipping open her purse, Norma took out a small wrapped package and handed it to Mary Ann. "Merry Christmas to you too."

Mary Ann blushed as she whispered her thanks.

"Shall I lock the door?" said Norma, as she walked out.

"No, you go ahead. I'll be right behind you." Mary Ann sprinted toward the door, catching up with Norma to give her a hug. As the chime of the doorbell announced Norma's departure, Mary Ann locked the door and flipped the 'Closed' sign.

Chapter 2

CONNOR WATCHED MARY Ann gather her coat and purse. His hopes of any reconciliation faded as he realized she was about to leave. Before his return, Connor had indulged in visions of their meeting—how she'd be whooping and jumping, then running straight into his arms. She would have a wide, drawn-out smile, her long hair flowing. In his mind, he would repeat the sequence. This time in slow motion. The bounce of her soft curls, eyes shining and bright, mouth slightly parted, with lips the color of red velvet …

"Connor, what's wrong?"

He shook his head as the image quickly faded. Sighing, he exhaled a deep breath. Here was his chance to tell her. It was now or never. "I'm sorry." He raised his eyes, meeting her square-on. "I'm so sorry I didn't call." He paused. "I was in my own funk, dealing with my life—what's left of it."

She remained silent, waiting for him to continue.

"After I went back to the city, I thought of you. I've picked up the phone." He hesitated again. "You have no idea how many times I tried to call you."

She played with the curl in her hair, twirling it as her feelings went into turmoil.

"But it wasn't the right time. I needed time to heal. I had to mourn … I needed to find myself." Connor fidgeted, shifting the weight on his feet.

"Look, I know you had a lot to deal with," said Mary Ann. "Your mother—"

"Going away, I thought it would dampen the pain. But it deepened it."

"I worried about you. Didn't know if you made it back or if you were okay." She stuck her chin out. She omitted the part where she was disappointed that he hadn't called.

"It was wrong of me. I didn't mean to cause you to worry." Connor shook his head.

She fiddled with the metal pull on the zipper of her purse—feeling its smoothness; flipping it back and forth.

"These last four months or so, I needed time for myself," said Connor. "I had no right to bring you into my world. I was barely functioning, as it was. I had days … well, weeks, when I felt I had nothing more to live for."

Mary Ann looked down, intent on hiding the flush of her cheeks, as her anger ebbed.

"I kept to myself," Connor whispered. "I made myself go through the motions of living, barely making it through each day. I failed poor Tom."

The mention of Tom, his orange tabby cat, brought a

smile to her lips. "And how is Tom?"

"He's not his usual self. I'm a little worried about him," said Connor, frowning. "I'm afraid something is wrong. I've neglected him. I was so absorbed in my own self."

"I'll give you the name of my vet," said Mary Ann. "That is, if you're still around after the holidays."

"Sure, I'd like that," said Connor. He added, softly. "Tom lost some weight."

"You'll still be here?"

Connor nodded.

Mary Ann reached across the counter for the notepad, scribbling the name and number of her vet. She tore the sheet off, and folded it. "You give him a call."

Connor took the paper. He smiled, as he read it. "Doc Carlson—so he's still around. He was Tom's vet before."

"He's the only vet in town," said Mary Ann.

"My mother took Tom to see him after the cat showed up at her doorstep one day."

"She had a soft spot for animals."

"Mom had a big heart."

"Your mother … she was kind to me when I first moved here. After I opened my flower shop, she was one of my first customers." Mary Ann gestured, waving her arm across the room. "I didn't know it at the time, but she had spread the word to all her friends, and they came."

"I appreciated the beautiful flower arrangements you made for her funeral."

"It was the least I could do."

Connor reached out to touch her hand. The barest of

contact. Perhaps he imagined it—a connection; an exchange of electrons sizzling in the air, bridging the gap.

Had she felt it, the tiny spark? It was like a weight had lifted—a clearing starting to open. Just a little.

Chapter 3

SEEING CONNOR COME home when his mom died had stirred up raw emotions Mary Ann had buried. The fact he grieved so openly. The loss which could never be replaced. How could one ever get over that?

Mary Ann fought back tears for the loneliness of her own life; for the special somebody to love and live her life with, to share her dreams, to comfort her in times of need. Who would grieve her when she died? She yearned to bare her most innermost feelings—her deepest, most soul-wrenching secrets, and desires. But not just to anyone. She would save it for the right somebody.

That day, four months ago, during Mrs. Norton's funeral, she sat in the church, lost in the breathtakingly beautiful music. It flowed in the air, expanding beyond the pews and vaulting to the ceiling of the church, enveloping her in a rapture-like state. Oblivious to anything and anyone else, she stared at Connor while the duet of flute and violin played. The heavenly music swirled, touching her soul. She was unable to tear her eyes away. Caught in the moment when time stood still. She glimpsed it, briefly—not the ethereal beauty of the notes but what *he* felt, deep inside.

How could she explain it? It was more than empathy and compassion. Shivers ran through her then, as they did now. It was as if she *was* part of it, the intersection of life and death before time pulled one into the beyond; before death took someone further and further away. She knew no matter how fast she ran after Death carrying a beloved away, trying to catch them—the speck of vision, their retreating figures, would get smaller and smaller. Eventually, she would run out of breath and collapse on the ground.

The chords of music brought her back. Brought Connor back.

In that instant, she had traveled with him, down the road one day everyone would travel. But it wasn't their time. Not for Connor. Not for Mary Ann.

Chapter 4

MAIN STREET AT Christmas was Connor's favorite time. Standing outside Mary Ann's flower shop, he looked down the street. Where could he go? The thought of seeing Mary Ann had consumed his mind during the drive down here from the city. He had made no plans for afterward.

The night before, Connor had paid his respects to his parents at the cemetery, leaving a bouquet of white flowers he brought from the city. Early this morning, on Christmas Eve, he fed Tom, then got in his car and drove straight to the flower shop to see Mary Ann. His mind had played a warm welcome over and over, like in the movies—smiling, arms flung wide open and hugs so tight you could hardly breathe.

It didn't happen like that. The disappointment was tough to bear. But the welcome he had imagined was of Connor's own making. Connor let out a deep breath. He watched as it blew into the cold—making its presence known—and then disappeared. He looked around the brightly decorated town and the busy street. This was Christmas Eve. Where was everyone going? They *all* had a place to go.

His eyes took in the red bows, wrapped around the lamp posts, the strung lights, the hustle and bustle of last-minute shoppers scurrying, carrying bags and boxes.

Connor noticed how much the town had changed. Christmas shopping wasn't like this when he was growing up. They could barely afford it. But he never felt poor. When his mother asked him what he wanted for Christmas, he'd name one thing. A teddy bear, when he was small; a toy train when he got older. His parents somehow managed his one present every year. He was never greedy. Even at a young age, he knew if he had asked for a more expensive item, he would set himself up for disappointment. As soon as he was old enough, Connor did odd jobs around town, earning enough to buy a used bicycle. And with it, he got a job delivering newspapers.

Across the street, the coffee shop beckoned as porch lights twinkled and a warm glow inside beamed its welcome. He caught a glimpse of customers enjoying mugs of steaming coffee, laughing and having a good time. Connor gathered his coat about him, feeling the wintry chill. He was drawn toward the light from a window, warm and inviting. Before he could think too much about it, his feet were marching to the coffee shop.

Holiday music played as Connor made his way to the counter to order—a jazzed-up rendition of "Jingle Bells."

Colorful paintings lined the walls, accompanied by white square signs with the name of the artist and the price. Bold landscapes, pastel flowers, portraits, a yellow van covered with love and peace signs. The café had a brash, artsy atmosphere.

For sure, it wasn't a chain coffee house. This one had a uniqueness to it—a quirky, small-town flavor. The tables were made of wood and each crafted by hand in a woodworking shop. No cookie-cutter, coated plywood tables here.

He scrutinized the menu on the chalkboard. Somebody with an artistic flair had outdone themselves. White, evergreen, and holly-red cursive lettering announced the featured specials. "Gingerbread latte topped with …" said Connor, squinting his eyes.

"Peppermint," a voice said.

Connor stared at the person in front of him; at the back of their head and the close-cropped hair. A man, he guessed. A short man, at least eight inches shorter than him. But the voice … it was different, not so masculine.

Connor bent down to whisper. "How about reading the dessert menu?"

"You're not that helpless!" The person laughed, turning around to face him.

The face was definitely not masculine. It looked familiar, yet Connor couldn't place it. "I know you …"

She smiled.

"Wait, don't tell me. Let me think," said Connor, snapping his fingers.

"You're Connor, aren't you?"

"Just give me a minute."

"What'll you have?" said the cashier, breaking in. The line had moved, and they were next.

"I'll have a cup of hot chocolate," said the person in front of him, moving up to the counter. "Oh, and I'd like some mini marshmallows."

"You're Alana!" said Connor, smiling in triumph as he finally put a name to the face.

He caught the attention of the cashier before Alana could pay. "Put it on my bill, please. I'll have your holiday special, the gingerbread latte." Connor pointed at the menu board.

"I do recommend it," she said, giving him an approving look. "For here or to go?"

"For here, please." Connor turned to Alana before she had time to thank him. "Care to join me?" He moved quickly to grab a table that had just emptied.

Noting her nod, Connor pulled out a chair for her, before going back for their drinks.

He sat the steaming mugs on the table.

"I guess I can stay for a few minutes," said Alana.

They shared a moment of silence, interrupted by a spoon clinking as Alana stirred her hot chocolate.

Connor studied her face, carefully. "It's been a long time." He straightened up in his seat and took another sip of his latte. "My neighbor, Mrs. Rainer, had an only child … a daughter."

"You're right. I'm Dottie's daughter, Alana."

"I knew you growing up, but I haven't seen you for years," said Connor.

"I've been away."

"You left home suddenly. I heard something happened, but I didn't know what. Mrs. Rainer hasn't spoken of you since."

"It's a long story … and I'd rather not go into it now."

Alana was silent, turning to stare out the window.

"How long has it been since you left?"

"It was eight years ago. I'm twenty-five now," said Alana. The man in front of her was no longer the thin, pimply kid he'd once been.

"I'm thirteen years older than you," said Connor.

Alana nodded. So, sitting across from her was a thirty-eight-year-old smooth-shaven, well-groomed and self-assured man. "Before I left, I saw you, what, maybe a couple times a year, when you came back to visit? It seems so long ago."

"Every time I came home, you'd spurted a few inches," said Connor, smiling as he recalled the little girl next door, shooting up like a thin, straight stalk.

"I left when I was seventeen, after Dad died." Alana shrugged, adding, "You know, the rebellious teenager and all the drama of growing up and figuring out who you are, and—"

"You had a lot to deal with."

"I had it rough on my own. I was almost homeless," said Alana. "I toughened up quick. I became a fast learner. I had to survive." She blew on the hot chocolate, pursing her thin lips, before taking another sip. "Tell me about you."

"I left here right after high school at eighteen. Moved to

the city, took classes at the community college, then transferred to the state college."

"You graduate?"

"*Cum laude.* Then I got a corporate job working in business and technology."

Alana noted his haircut—precise and perfectly cut. She imagined it was probably like his life, all neat and in order, packaged and tied up in a bow. Was Connor's life safe and predictable? Had he ever taken chances? Was he happy? He had the look of success. Even dressed casually, his sleek-fitting fighter pilot jacket screamed designer label. Where the jacket was unzipped, she could see a black turtleneck sweater underneath. She slid a glance at her outfit: the cheap winter jacket from Wally World, the plain cotton shirt, the thermal underwear under it, and the well-worn pair of jeans. Alana touched her chest, fingers grazing the natural, soft fabric of her shirt.

"So, here you are, back in town, on Christmas Eve," said Connor after a moment of silence. The guilt of his infrequent visits home weighed heavily on his mind, brought back by the conversation with Alana.

"I just got in today. I can't believe how much it's changed in eight years."

"A few new stores have popped up. But at the core, it's still the same place and people."

"I passed the old theater and the marquee advertising 'The Nutcracker'."

"The *same* movie they show every year, I bet."

"My mom took me to see the show when I was in first

grade," said Alana. "We went a few times, but when I turned twelve, I refused to go."

"It was a tradition in our house too. Thankfully, I only went twice with my mother," chuckled Connor.

"The dry cleaner is still here. It's as drab-looking as I remembered it." Alana stuck her tongue out and made a funny face.

"They must do good business," said Connor. "I remember they delivered to our house every two weeks, on Tuesday."

"Oh yeah, I know that delivery truck. It had a gigantic picture of a clothes hanger on the side."

Connor smiled. "My mother sent my dad's shirts out to be dry-cleaned. Of course, he fussed at first. He didn't see a need in it. But she was insistent that he looked every bit the owner of his hardware store."

"Did he?"

"She insisted, and in the end, he agreed and let her. Mother was particular about clothes, always checking me and nagging me about mine."

"Even I could tell she had style," said Alana, wishing it was a talent her own mom had.

"Mom managed to look fashionable. She had a knack for matching and mixing outfits. It didn't need to be expensive—she did it with what we had."

It felt good—sitting in the small coffee shop, all toasty and warm, a mug of delicious warm drink at hand, talking to Alana. Connor didn't want to get into anything that would ruin the mood and was relieved Alana didn't seem to, either. As to why she left town, according to rumors, something happened, and it wasn't good. Going over and rehashing past hurts would be upsetting.

Connor sat back in his chair and smiled. "I'm glad you're back in town. Imagine running into you in the coffee shop."

"I dashed in to grab something warm. You're the first familiar face I've seen since I drove into town."

"You haven't seen your mother, yet …?"

"I stopped for gas, then came in here."

Connor twirled his spoon, scooping up a bit of foam on top. He had plenty of room to slosh around, having drunk half of the latte already. "You know my mother died."

She nodded. "Your mother, she was a good person and kind to me." Alana reached across the table to grasp Connor's hand. "I'm so sorry for your loss."

Connor swallowed, feeling the familiar ache that didn't rear its ugly head as often now. It was, but nevertheless, still there, and might never go away. "I miss her terribly. Coming home for the holidays will never be the same."

She squeezed his hand, covering it with her palm.

He looked up at her, his eyes tearing up. "I don't know what happened between you and your mother. Forget it, bury the ill feelings. Make up with her—while you still have her."

Chapter 5

Eight years ago

IT WAS THREE-THIRTY in the morning when she got up from the bed, dressed, and quietly gathered the rest of her clothes and toiletries, stuffing them in the carry-on and backpack. As she stepped into the hall, Alana paused outside her mother's room. It was quiet. In the dim light, she had crept slowly on her sock-covered feet, making her way to the kitchen. She held the envelope in her hands. Enclosed was a brief note:

> *I'm leaving. Please don't look for me.*
> *Alana*

She placed it in the middle of the kitchen counter, where her mom would be sure to see it in the morning.

Alana looked around the living room—the simple furniture, the scuffed-up wooden floor, the round rug under the coffee table with a stain in the corner from fruit juice she spilled when she was a toddler.

This had been home to her for seventeen years. It was the only home she had ever known. It was scary, what she was about to do. She sighed. It wasn't too late. She could still go back to her room and crawl back under the comfy covers.

She shook her head. It had been her decision, and she was going to go through with it. Zipping up her jacket, Alana tiptoed to the front door, turned the knob, opened the door and walked out. This time, she didn't turn around.

Now, Alana was back on Christmas Eve. The little town had changed a bit, with new stores and businesses. Alana hadn't seen her mother for all that time. Had the years been kind to her? After she left, Alana had refused to call home for help. She was as stubborn as can be. The last thing she'd ever do was admit she had made a mistake.

Why did she come back? Mrs. Norton's death had something to do with it. Alana missed the funeral. By the time she found out, it was too late to change her plans. Pastor Maller had been kind. He was really the only connection she maintained. She trusted him. He didn't blame her or judge her. He never yelled at her or said hurtful words. He was a man of God, and he took that mantle on. She took refuge with his kindness.

Alana had imagined the meeting with her mother—practiced what she'd say, over and over again. She had chosen her words carefully.

She was tired. Tired of the freezing nights she shivered in

her little room, not much bigger than a closet. Tired of the cold that a warm bowl of soup could soothe only for a moment. Tired of begging for money. Tired of lying, cheating, doing whatever she had to do to survive. Tired of gagging on the taste of crusted urine and the smell of body odor when she performed oral sex on strange men. Tired of living, sometimes.

Tired of being so tired. And worried. Worried about catching some disease and becoming ill. Worried about dying alone in some forsaken place. Alana plunged to the depths of despair in a harsh world, so different from the one she understood. Yet she kept on living, not giving up. Her stubborn self refused to give up.

One day, she stumbled on a park. The benches were free, and she could sit and get plenty of sunshine. She chose a warm spot with a good view. She could sit there for hours, and nobody would bother her. Old people liked to go there. Alana liked old people, and she liked talking to them. They had stories. In the twilight of their years, they spoke of their lives, of people they loved and lost. Some confessed their secrets, regrets and longings. They told her while they still could—before everything was forgotten; before they had no more stories to tell; before their voices were stilled.

It was on one of those days she felt so moved. The stories stirred up feelings deep inside, and it dawned on her that she should be writing. She couldn't keep them shoved down. She began on the computer in the library. She took a thumb drive with her and saved her words. She blogged about her life—being penniless and her struggles to survive. Each day was a new adventure. The writing fueled her life, and her life fueled her writing.

Writing became her constant companion, a testament to her will to survive. She laid her gritty life bare for all to read. Little by little, her audience grew, as word spread and people sought out her blogs. Her style was distinct. It was edgy and raw.

She grew a following, as more people waited for the next chapter of her life. After several months, she compiled her blogs. It was one of her online followers who suggested she publish it. She was able to barter for services online: an editor, a graphic designer to do her book cover for cheap. Using free software, she formatted and published it. Her followers spread the word and bought her book. It seemed like an overnight success, but it wasn't. She had grown her readership slowly, bit by bit. It hadn't been easy at all.

Chapter 6

Four months ago

CONNOR HAD FIRST met Mary Ann, four months ago, at her flower shop, when he came back in town to discuss arrangements for his mother's funeral. He ran into her again, later, and invited her over for a home-cooked meal with family friends. They dined at Manini's before Connor returned to his home in the city. Connor had thought of calling Mary Ann. Well, it had crossed his mind many a time. He had reached for the phone to call her, he didn't. Deep down, Connor felt ashamed and didn't want to use her as a crutch—something to ease his own misery. He didn't want to burden another human being. Not just anyone, either, but someone who had been kind to him and his mother. And someone who he liked. He wasn't proud of himself. He didn't want her to see him like this. Not Mary Ann.

Four months ago, Connor had gone back to the city. At work, they had given him some slack at first, but how far could it go? Pretty soon, the sympathies ran short, and he wasn't doing his job well. Connor had cashed in on some favors, and there were many, but that ran dry. People distanced themselves from him. Even the ones he thought were his friends avoided him.

Then, sitting behind his desk, looking out the clear glass pane of the window, seeing blue sky on this cloudless day, Connor knew the day would come when he'd have to give up his coveted window office—the one he worked for years to attain. But he was a proud man. He hadn't and wouldn't simply give up. Not without a fight. Not unless it was under his terms.

Before he left the city, Connor had turned in his resignation. He was done with his job. His bosses had wanted him to come back, for a going away party, but he told them 'no'. He thanked them but held firm to his decision. He was adamant about ending his life in the city and beginning the new year in his home town. He'd start with a clean slate. He had enough money saved up, from socking his money away every payday. This money was meant for retirement, but this felt like the right thing to do with it.

He'd interviewed a few real estate agents about putting up his condo for sale. The suggestions they made were minor—cosmetic touches. Connor sold his furniture and put the rest of his stuff in the back of his SUV. He didn't need much. Most of his clothes—the shirts and suits—went to the church donation center, down the street. Little by little, he bundled clothes, shoes, and other items and took them there. Each step he took, he felt lighter, as he shed more stuff. In the end, at his last stop, he celebrated.

Chapter 7

Two months ago

MARY ANN RECALLED the first time she met Ron. He dropped by the flower shop two months ago, during her lunch break. It was mid-week, on a slow day. They struck up a conversation about plants. It was an interest they had in common, as it turned out. Ron was the new owner of the hardware store. He wanted to expand the outdoor section, adding a garden center with plants.

Mary Ann felt his energy and his excitement, and she was flattered when he invited her to visit his store. She chalked it up to a networking opportunity with another small business owner—a chance to bounce ideas back and forth.

The next day, Mary Ann drove to his store while Norma minded the flower shop. It was early afternoon. Pulling into the parking lot, she spotted Ron immediately. He was busy loading concrete blocks and bundles of chopped wood on a customer's flatbed. It was a chilly day, only slightly warmed by the afternoon sun, but he wore a cotton shirt and jeans.

She waited, watching him work while she leaned against the side of her car.

Apparently, he had noticed her too. He walked toward her as the loaded truck pulled away.

Mary Ann watched as Ron approached, crossing the parking lot in long, easy strides. He looked relaxed, not dawdling when he was going someplace where he wanted to be. His hair was disheveled. His plaid shirt was unbuttoned at the top. It clung to his body, plastered with sweat. In jeans, his hips and legs were slim. The rolled-up shirt sleeves provided a glimpse of arms with corded muscles that extended down to strong hands and long fingers.

"Hi, Mary Ann," Ron said, wiping his palm on his jeans before reaching out to shake her hand. She kept her eyes on him as he grabbed a cloth sticking up in his back pocket and wiped his forehead.

"Catch you at a bad time?"

"Nah." Ron shook his head, grinning. The breeze ruffled his hair, giving him a slightly wild look.

"Well," she said, stopping to straighten out an imaginary wrinkle on her skirt. "I see you're a hands-on kinda guy."

Ron burst out laughing, lines crinkling on his rugged face. "You're right about that."

She smiled back. As much as she liked working in her flower shop, getting out today had turned into a pleasant distraction. She had found the hardware store easily, having stopped there briefly once before for a quick purchase. She hadn't run into Ron, that time.

Mary Ann needed to get a life. She couldn't help feeling

she was playing hooky today, standing in front of a self-assured and masculine man in his element. She was also cursing herself now for not paying attention to some past gossip about Ron. She couldn't recall anything that had been whispered about him. Mary Ann shook her head, dragging herself away from her thoughts and giving him her full attention.

"Would you like a tour of this place?"

"I'd love to see it."

He tilted his head toward the fenced enclosure near the back. "Let's go this way first."

Ron's face was lit with a goofy grin. His enthusiasm bubbled—he could barely contain himself. He gestured, pointing to the east corner. "I'd like to put the saplings here." Waving over to the side, he added, "The perennials could go there, and maybe some hanging flower baskets and a herb garden, or something fun for the kids."

Ron turned around to the other side. "Lawn mowers and weed whackers could go here. And maybe some outdoor furniture, if there's room."

Mary Ann had to walk fast to keep up with him. As Ron moved quickly indoors, she could hear the excitement in his voice. He was like an eager boy, showing off his treasured possessions. From the way he talked and acted, she could tell how proud he was. She could also see that he was someone who wasn't too proud to get his hands dirty—a man who did an honest day's work and felt good about it.

"This is how the store was when I bought it from Connor Norton's father," said Ron, leading the way to his office. "I'll show you the plans drawn for the expansion."

He opened the door and pulled out a chair for her to sit in front of his desk. He reached on top of the file cabinet for the rolled-up blueprint. He unfurled it, spreading it across the desktop, using rocks, a screwdriver, and a hammer to secure the corners. Gesturing to her to move closer, he pointed.

"See here?" He glanced at her to ensure he had her full attention. "I'm going to build an addition."

Ron pointed to the space behind the office. "On the other side of this wall, I'm going to add a new space, and put in the large appliances. Refrigerator, stove, washer and dryer." He traced the outline and tapped his finger on the blueprint. "Over here, I'm putting in a small appliances section. It'll be mostly kitchen appliances, fans, space heaters, and odds and ends."

"This isn't just a little remodeling. You're talking about a major expansion."

"This place needs it. I've been thinking about it for a long time now," said Ron. He was slightly hunched over the desk.

He turned to Mary Ann and stood up straight. "This is my dream, Mary Ann." He was staring at her now with an intensity that showed his determination.

"You've got the plans … What's there to stop you?"

Mary Ann wondered if it was the right thing to say, as his firmly-pressed lips appeared to weaken with just the barest twitch.

He ran his hands over his hair. *Damn, she'd nailed it on the head.* What *was* stopping him?

Ron had mentioned his plans to Connor, when he came back in town for his mother's funeral. Ron had put it out to him, then—he made the offer to Connor first, to partner fifty-fifty to expand Connor's family's old hardware store. Connor wanted to think it over. Ron gave him more time and told Connor he wanted an answer within the year.

Twenty years earlier, Connor had left town after high school, much to the disappointment of his parents. Mr. Norton had hoped his son would take over the family business and work at the hardware store, but he couldn't compete with the pull of the big city and the promises it offered to the ambitious young man. In the end, when the elder Mr. Norton could no longer work, he sold the business to Ron, who had worked for him for over ten years.

From the beginning, Ron had absorbed every aspect of the business and hungered for more. He started out mopping floors and cleaning the toilet, or whatever else Mr. Norton wanted him to do. Along the way, he learned, soaking up everything he could. When a customer came in and had a question, if Ron didn't know the answer then he'd find out. Ron never gave a bullshit response. He'd persist until he could give proper advice. Not a flimsy, carelessly-thrown reply, but a serious, thoughtful one. The customer never forgot. It wasn't just the customer who was satisfied, oddly enough; Ron had a feeling of accomplishment and tucked the new knowledge under his hat.

Ron had gone with his gut feeling, asking Mary Ann to come here. What was he thinking of, sharing his dreams of expansion with her? Mary Ann was a businesswoman—gutsy, hard-working and smart. More than that, deep down, he admired what she had done. He decided to trust his instincts.

"For starters, money," said Ron. "I made an offer to someone, to become equal partners."

"Did they take you up on it?" Mary Ann raised an eyebrow, surprised at the generosity of the offer.

Ron shook his head. "I gave him till the end of the year … but I haven't got an answer yet."

"Well, you don't have much time left. Why is he taking so long?"

"You'll have to ask him," said Ron. He had been patient, but waiting until the last minute wasn't a good way to start off a partnership, albeit a very generous one.

"Him? Do I know this person?"

Ron took a hard look at her. *Should he confide in her? Hadn't he told her too much, already?* "You want to know?"

She nodded, not wanting to appear too interested, but she was curious.

"You know Connor Norton?"

Mary Ann gasped. *Connor!*

Ron felt relief, as he shared the information with her. It had been weighing down on him for a good while. He wasn't in his right mind to give Connor this long to decide. Ron did it out of respect for Mrs. Norton, and her son who had been overwhelmed by grief at the loss of his mother.

"He'd better get in touch with me, or the deal is off," said Ron.

"What's this section?" asked Mary Ann, hiding the blush on her face as she bent over the blueprint, pointing to a large corner space.

"The bathrooms."

"I hope you're remodeling a nice big one for the ladies."

He grunted. "Now, *that* I hadn't thought of. Maybe I'll put in some fancy fixtures."

Mary Ann liked that idea.

Chapter 8

December 24

MARY ANN SWUNG into the parking space. Pumping the gas pedal for the uphill climb, the car had spewed flying gravel on the driveway. Ron had texted, asking her to meet him at the hardware store again. His business had stayed open, closing later on Christmas Eve than her flower shop.

Mary Ann grasped the collar of her coat, closing the gap against the wind. It was an unconscious act, out of habit. Her other hand was flung across her waist.

A couple of weeks ago, Ron had casually mentioned something about Christmas, telling Mary Ann he was going to head out to his cabin. It was small but quaint—a cozy, rustic place. He had asked Mary Ann if she'd be interested in joining him.

"A day trip, and we'd be back by evening?" said Mary Ann.

"Yes, and if the weather is good, we could do some hiking."

"So, it's not too far."

"About an hour away," said Ron.

Mary Ann had hesitated.

"Now, when's the last time you took some time off?" Ron pressed.

"I have so much to do, to be invested in my work, but—"

"But what? You couldn't get away?"

"Right. I didn't have any help. But now, with Norma as my assistant, it's taken a load off."

"Have you seen much of this place, outside of town?"

Mary Ann shook her head.

"I grew up here. I'll drive you around. We'll stop at the cabin, have lunch, then head on back to town."

Ron waited, then nudged her for a response. "So, how about it? If we end up with a white Christmas, it'll be even prettier."

Mary Ann found herself considering his invite.

"Do you have plans?" Ron kept his voice low-key and casual.

"Norma has invited me over to her place for supper, if I didn't have other plans," said Mary Ann.

"You have a couple of offers, then. Just keep in mind that mine is going to be more fun." Ron winked, flashing the most charming smile he could muster.

"Okay, okay, I accept!" Mary Ann laughed.

"You lucked out today. Got the last one," said Ron, grinning. "And you're my last customer on Christmas Eve."

"I'm sure glad you had this," said the man, as he fumbled in his pants pocket for his wallet.

"Let me ring you up," said Ron. He lifted the tree stand and scanned the bar-coded label, as Mary Ann stepped inside the hardware store.

"My family will have their Christmas after all." The man sighed with relief, thinking of the cut fir in his truck. "Whoever invented this tree stand is a genius. A piece of plastic with screws to hold up the tree. Santa will be leaving presents under this tree tonight."

The man carried the tree stand as he crossed the room, giving a thank-you nod as he went out the front door. He carefully side-stepped the pile of dirt that the high school kid had swept off the floor. The kid chased the debris again, as a gust of wind rushed in and pushed it along the pinewood floor.

"Joey, go home," said Ron, catching sight of his employee's exasperated look.

"Seriously?"

Ron reached in the cash drawer and pulled out an envelope containing Joey's weekly wages. "I want you to enjoy Christmas with your family."

The kid took the envelope and looked inside. "There's an extra hundred in here," he gasped. He looked at Ron, then at the envelope, and then at Mary Ann.

Ron shook his head, gesturing toward the door. "Now, get going before I change my mind."

"Thank you, sir," beamed Joey. He had been brought up right and proper by his mama. She'd taught him his good manners.

Ron watched Joey walk outside, the top of his head bobbing further away as he weaved down the hill. Something about the kid reminded him of himself, a long time ago.

Ron strode across the room and flipped the door sign to 'Closed.' His steps echoed in the quiet hardware store with just the two of them.

He walked back to Mary Ann.

"Hey, you all right?"

"Just lost in thought," said Mary Ann, as she blinked her eyes.

"A penny for your thoughts?"

"It'll cost you more."

"Ouch," said Ron, pretending to hold on to his wallet.

"Give it up." Mary Ann laughed, playfully tugging his arm.

"Ready for tomorrow's outing?"

"Tell me what I need to bring."

"Just bring yourself and bundle up. Wear a good pair of hiking boots."

"What time are we leaving?"

"I'll pick you up at eight in the morning."

Mary Ann groaned. "It's so early."

"Let's go for 8:30 a.m. and call it a compromise," said Ron, with a tease to his voice.

"Not on Christmas Day!"

"Okay, then—nine."

"That's better."

"We can still hike and work up a good appetite before noon."

Mary Ann couldn't help wondering if Ron had something else in mind, besides hiking.

Chapter 9

NOW, THE HOUSE sat empty on Christmas Eve. It was bare of holiday decorations. It was devoid of all holiday spirit, since Connor's mom died.

Stores were closing early. By two o'clock in the afternoon, the pickings were sparse, but Connor managed to grab some outside lights, a few decorations, and a misshapen, pathetic-looking fir tree, which had been pushed into a corner and overlooked by shoppers. "A tree has to have something under it," his mother always said. Connor picked up some special treats and toys for Tom, along with some wrapping paper.

He stopped by the market and bought milk, eggs, fresh vegetables and fruits, and enough food to stock his refrigerator for a few days.

Coming home … He hadn't given it much thought until he was well on the way. Getting into the holiday spirit had been the last thing on his mind. He just wanted to relax on the couch and be left alone with Tom.

But walking in the festive town, caught up in the hustle and bustle, checking out the Christmas decorations, lights, music, food and drinks … it all affected Connor. Despite himself, he found a little holiday cheer wrapping around his heart.

In the end, he gave in and embraced it. For himself. And for what his mother would have wanted for him—to go on and join life, rather than retreat from it. To be happy. It would have been easy to withdraw and do nothing. It took energy to do something. All of this—the latte, the talk with Alana, getting caught in the holiday spirit of this small town where he grew up and where his parents were laid to rest—wasn't what he had planned.

He suddenly realized he wasn't ready to give up. He felt charged with a renewed energy and excitement he hadn't felt since he was a child.

The rest of the afternoon passed quickly, as Connor busied himself putting lights outside the house and decorating the inside. The Christmas tree in the living room was the centerpiece. There was a cloth on the floor beneath it, with a few wrapped gifts scattered on top—mainly cat treats and toys for Tom.

He picked up Tom when he finished trimming, taking a walk around the living room to survey his work. Flicking the lights on, he walked outside, giving a satisfied grunt as the blinking holiday lights and glow of colors brightened the unassuming bland exterior of the house.

"See, Tom?" said Connor, as he held the cat's paw and waved it.

Connor was determined to enjoy the holidays together with Tom and family friends, spreading the cheer. Tom had endured a rough time too, and Connor had been selfish. He'd devoted time to his job, while being preoccupied with feeling sorry for himself. Connor wanted to make it up to Tom. Tom was all the family he had left—his mother's orange tabby cat. *His* cat.

In the end, it was family that mattered.

Chapter 10

IN THE EVENING, Connor attended the Christmas Eve candlelight service at the church. It was something he hadn't done by himself since he left home.

Going to the service had been a tradition when he was a child. Every year, he went with his parents.

Returning to the church brought back so many childhood memories of that time. Before the service started, a candle with paper drip guards was passed out to each person. The simple act of lighting the candles filled the congregation with reverence. When he got older, he was allowed his own candle. He cupped his hands around the flickering flame to prevent it from being snuffed by a draft. It was a solemn yet inspiring moment, made more so when the whole congregation did it together—the beauty of candle lights shining in the darkened sanctuary, bringing the message of hope and peace. It stirred up memories of sitting between his parents, and of the wonder he felt as a child.

The Pastor gave his welcome, embracing everyone—even those who only attended services twice a year, at Christmas and Easter. Connor grimaced, putting himself in that category. In the twenty years since he'd been away, Connor had become one of them—ever since his eighteenth birthday, when he learned the truth about his adoption—by the man whom he called "Dad", growing up. The man who was not his biological father, after all. Connor took it hard. Choked with anger and resentment for two decades, he had avoided coming home as much as possible. But now, as he sat back on the familiar pews and listened to the Pastor, he was at peace. He touched his mother's letter, which he put in his coat pocket after opening and reading it the day before. There, on December twenty-third, at the cemetery where she rested next to his adoptive father, Connor learned the truth about the man who married his pregnant mother.

He stayed awhile after the church service, to thank Pastor Maller and greet town folks he knew. It was good to see the Pastor again—and his daughter, Eva. He hadn't seen them since the funeral.

Spotting Mrs. Rainer leaving, Connor rushed after her. He caught up with her on the lawn.

She tapped his arm, affectionately. "Good to see you home."

"How've you been?"

"You know me—the feisty old woman next door isn't going anywhere."

Connor looked around, hoping to see Alana. He hesitated, not wanting to be the one to ask Mrs. Rainer about her daughter. He thought, *She doesn't know yet about Alana.*

"Merry Christmas, Mrs. Rainer."

"You call me Dottie, and you too."

Connor suddenly had an idea. "Dottie, I have some people over tomorrow for an early Christmas supper. It's nothing fancy. A simple meal. You're invited." Connor gave her a warm hug. "Can you come at two?"

Mrs. Rainer visibly brightened, her eyes shining as she smiled. "Thank you for the invitation, Connor. I'd be delighted. It'll be good to see Tom too. How is he?"

"Tom is fine, although I'm a little worried because he's lost some weight."

"Have you taken him to the vet?"

"In the city. I've got the number of the vet to call in town."

She nodded. "Doc Carlson? Your mother went to him, as well."

"Yes, I know Doc Carlson. I'll be taking Tom there."

⁓⸺❦⸺⁓

As he sat on the couch, with Tom curled next to him, Connor closed his eyes. He remembered how much he used to look forward to his mother's delicious homemade cookies after church, when they arrived back at the house. As a child, he believed these special cookies were for Santa, to be left by the chimney with a glass of milk. Later, he knew better, and by then he felt no remorse, when eating 'Santa's cookies.'

The thought of his mother's mouthwatering treats brought out a pang which came from nowhere, stunning him, as he tried to hold back sudden tears.

Milk and cookies. Laughter. Music. Perhaps, if he tried hard enough, he would catch a whiff of aroma from the oven, as cookies baked in the kitchen, or hear the sounds of music from times gone by.

～ܢܫ܀ܫܢ～

Connor reached for his cell phone, scrolling down until he found the number.

She picked up on the first ring.

"Alana, this is Connor." He came right to the point. "I went to church tonight. Your mother was there."

"What's wrong?"

"I didn't see you there. You haven't talked to your mother, have you?"

She hesitated. "No, but I'm thinking about going to see her on Christmas Day."

"Have you made a decision about coming over for an early supper? I've invited your mother, and she's coming."

There was a long pause on the other end, before Alana spoke. "Does she know I'm here?"

"I haven't mentioned it yet."

"Do you think that's a good idea? To … surprise her like this?"

"Couldn't hurt, could it? I mean, what would you rather do?"

"I've been waiting for the right time."

"Think about it. Sleep on it overnight."

Connor tapped the screen to end the call. He held the phone, his finger raised, frozen in space. Should he, or shouldn't he, call Mary Ann? The meeting at the flower shop hadn't played out like his dreams. She wasn't overjoyed to see him … but she wasn't cold, either. Was it too late to call her? To make amends? He sat back on the couch, his head resting on the sidearm, closing his eyes. He'd messed up.

Chapter 11

December 25

CONNOR WOKE UP to the familiar blue walls of his childhood bedroom. He lingered, for a moment, between reality and the land of dreams and memories. His groggy mind hadn't yet grasped where he was—he wasn't fully awake. Any minute now, his mom would be calling him to go down to breakfast. He felt loved and safe at home, in his own bed, the innocence of childhood not yet blemished. He relished the comfort of his bed, amongst the familiarity of the house he grew up in. His mind paused in the dimension where time stood still. In it, he went back thirty years. He held on to this innocence, not wanting to let it go. He willed his consciousness to stay in that realm.

The alarm on his cell phone shattered the silence, abruptly bringing Connor to the present. Reality set in, as he comprehended the moment, roughly snatching away the past he had dwelled in. It felt like there was nothing his mind could cling to—hold on to—as the clarity of the day replaced the dreamy realm he had occupied, moments before.

Connor felt the aches of grief, stabbing and jabbing him. At times, anger reared its head, at the thought of this unfairness—this loss in his life. The past few months had been difficult. For days, all he wanted to do was linger in bed. He felt like giving in to the sadness and letting it take over. The strength seeped out of him. This constant cycle of feelings felt like a worn-out tape, replayed over and over. On days like this, it was hard to get up and go to work. Back in the city, on days like this, he'd call in sick, relieved he had saved up hundreds of hours of sick time in lieu. He had never expected to have to use them in that way—that he'd relinquish the desire to work, exchanging it with the stronger pull to stay in bed.

He picked up the cell phone, glancing at the date displayed. December twenty-fifth.

Tom's whiskers tickled his face. Connor heard the soft sound of Tom's breathing, with its familiar nasal drone, right before he felt the wet spot of a feline nose, and the soft pads of Tom's front paws kneading on his chest.

Here, in the bedroom where he grew up, Tom was nestled on top of the blankets, his little body giving out heat. But what warmed Connor's heart was Tom's unconditional love.

Connor ruffled Tom's soft fur. He crooked his thumb under Tom's ears and scratched, right at his favorite spot. "Do you know what today is, Thomas?" When Connor wanted Tom to pay attention, this is what he'd call him.

"Me-ow," cried Tom. He rolled on his side, stretched his legs, and gave a huge yawn, mouth wide open.

Connor hugged Tom, holding his little body close.

Tom wriggled a bit, his intelligent green eyes wide open and ears perked up. His tongue flickered out to give a soft lick, then he got down to business, vigorously dampening his paws and rubbing his face and behind his ears. He repeated this over and over until his fur was wet, clumps of it sticking together. Finished with the task of washing his face, a well-groomed Tom strutted to the edge of the bed and jumped off.

"Hey, fella, let's go see what Santa has left for you," said Connor, bouncing off the mattress and hurrying after Tom.

Chapter 12

ON CHRISTMAS MORNING, Ron knocked on the door. He was punctual—right on time at nine in the morning. Mary Ann was drinking her coffee. She set her mug down and got up from the kitchen table to open the door.

Ron stood outside, all bundled up. Behind him, she could see his pickup truck.

"Merry Christmas, Ron. Come on in," said Mary Ann. Ron had previously fixed plumbing problems and electrical faults after hours at her flower shop. This was the first time he'd been to her home.

Ron wiped his shoes on the welcome mat and stepped inside. "Merry Christmas." He glanced around, noting the tastefully decorated living room. "Nice place you have here."

"I just made coffee. Would you like a cup?"

"I'll take it black," said Ron.

She poured a full cup and handed it to him, wisps of steam curling up. A white cat came out to investigate, sniffing him. "Oh, that's Isabella," said Mary Ann. "It's her way of saying 'hi'."

Ron reached down and held his hand out for her to smell, then petted her and scratched her back. He wasn't exactly a cat person, preferring the company of dogs. But he had no problem with cats, as long as they didn't scratch him.

Before long, they finished the coffee and were on their way to the cabin. Ron drove, eventually turning off onto a graveled forest road. Mary Ann wasn't used to the bumps and the rattling noise from the pickup, and the way Ron quick-tapped the brake. It reached the point where she felt nauseous. Mary Ann almost yelled for him to stop. If she had to puke by the side of the road, so be it.

Ron cranked up the radio, and it was hard to talk over the sound. This suited Mary Ann just fine. She held one hand over her mouth, in case a lurch flipped her stomach and made her throw up. Okay, it was gross. But feeling queasy like this was not good, either. She peeked at Ron. He was focused on driving and oblivious to her plight. She closed her eyes, signaling a 'Do not disturb' vibe his way. *One potato, two potatoes …* she chanted to herself, as she lulled to sleep, hoping that a quick nap would quiet her stomach and take her mind off the nausea.

Mary Ann felt a sharp poke in her arm—a great way to wake up. It put her in a lousy mood. She sat up, feeling the discomfort of the hard seat. She tried rubbing her neck, to relieve the cramped muscles.

They had stopped. The truck was parked in a gravel driveway. There was a log cabin a short distance away.

"We're here."

Mary Ann turned to Ron.

He was putting on his gloves. "Let's go."

"I can't wait to go inside!"

"Not so fast. We're going to take a walk first. I'll show you around the property and get the cabin heated up while you climb the mountain."

"What?" she practically screamed.

He laughed, tipping his head. "Just kidding. I think you need to climb out and stretch your legs first."

The door creaked loudly, as she pulled the handle to open it. The hinges were unforgiving and stiff.

"Hold on," said Ron, dashing to her side of the truck. He yanked the door handle, pulling the groaning door open. "I see what you mean. Man, I need to get this door fixed." He held out his hand, offering to lift her down.

"Just give me a moment," said Mary Ann. It was a chivalrous act but, being an independent woman, Mary Ann preferred to do it on her own. She was used to it. But she also liked being pampered and treated like a lady. What a delightful dilemma.

Ron stepped back, hands off. He watched as she gathered her stuff and swung her slim legs out. He chuckled to himself. His momma brought him up to be respectful and polite—ever the gentleman, especially where women were concerned. However, she also valued a woman who knew how to take care of herself. If she were alive today, he was sure she'd like Mary Ann.

Chapter 13

CONNOR LOVED THE crunch of carrots. He slipped a few pieces in his mouth—a cook's prerogative—as he sliced and diced tiny pieces for the salad. It had become a habit to have a salad with his meal, at least once a day. He added arugula, a must-have, due to its peppery, tasty flavor. Curious to learn more about this green, Connor found numerous benefits touted on the internet (ranging from weight loss to fighting cancers, as well as improvements in skin, bone, and brain health). He mixed in some romaine and baby kale, adding these greens for the nutritional value and variety.

By the time he'd built the salad, he'd added enough for a small mountain—plenty for the meal. He'd invited Pastor Maller and Eva, after the candlelight Christmas Eve service. With Mrs. Rainer, Alana, and himself, it would be five altogether. That is, it would be if Alana decided to come.

Mary Ann crossed his mind. Connor had texted her. He

wondered if she might still follow up. It was down to the wire. The chances of her attending this Christmas dinner were diminishing by the moment, his hopes of seeing her vanishing as disappointment swooped in to take its place.

Chapter 14

NEW SNOW HAD blanketed the ground with a layer of white. Mary Ann paused to take in the untouched beauty. *A white wonderland. A cabin nestled in the woods.* The crisp air turned her nose red. Bundled in layers of warm clothing, she welcomed Christmas Day, as the expelled air from her lungs breathed life into the cold, marking the presence of a living body.

Ron was in no hurry. He stood beside her, remembering the first time his dad had brought him out here. He was just a tyke. It was summertime, the verdant landscape showcasing the full bloom of beautiful wildflowers, tall, waving grass, and forested land.

Ron and Mary Ann stood in the now-wintry landscape, in comfortable silence, each lost in their own thoughts.

"My dad—he built this," said Ron, quietly.

Mary Ann nodded and waited for him to continue.

"The cabin used to be a campsite for hunters, but an

accident changed him and ended his hunting days." He paused. "My mom's always loved animals and never went hunting with my dad."

"When did this happen?" said Mary Ann, as she looked at the rustic cabin, trying to picture the man who built it.

"A long time ago, when I was a kid."

"Did he ever talk about that last time?"

"My dad said he had his sights on the deer. He was going to shoot the doe, then he saw her fawns in the background, moving closer to be with their mother. The doe raised her head. She was a beautiful doe with big brown eyes. As he raised his rifle to shoot, they locked eyes."

"And then?"

"He said, in that instant, he felt a change of heart. As he stood up from his crouched position, he lowered his rifle. Turning to walk back to the cabin, he tripped on a tangled branch on the ground, fell, and hurt himself. It was a serious injury."

"Oh, that's horrible."

"That's the last time he hunted."

"You still come up here with him?"

Ron shook his head. "He passed two years ago."

"I'm so sorry," said Mary Ann. He looked so forlorn she wanted to give him a hug. Instead, she reached out and patted his hand.

"They were married forty years." Ron didn't often act sentimental, at least not when he was at work. At the age of thirty-eight, he craved to find the kind of love his parents had. "My mother died six months later. She couldn't live without him."

Chapter 15

CONNOR RUBBED A circle on the kitchen window, clearing the steam from the glass pane. Outside, the yard was blanketed with snow. The bare branches of a tree were a stark contrast to the whiteness below. He missed his mom. For the first time in his thirty-eight years, he was spending Christmas alone, in the kitchen where his mother first taught him to cook; where they spent many happy hours together. She was gone forever. Staring at the dark tree, devoid of green leaves, he wondered for a moment if it was dead or still alive.

He felt something brush against his leg. The loud meow announced the presence of another living being. He was reminded he wasn't alone. Tom was with him. His mother had loved the cat. Now, it was his. Picking Tom up, Connor buried his face in the soft fur. "You old bugger, you know how much you mean to me."

Having Tom in his arms brought comfort and different

memories. Happy memories of holiday homecomings—his rosy-cheeked mom in her apron and the smell of herb-roasted potatoes in the oven. He could almost see the flickering flames in the fireplace, and hear soft laughter and music playing.

Connor made his first ornament in the kitchen with his mom. He was still a child and stood on a stepstool to reach over the counter top. Using ingredients in the pantry, they made salt dough baubles, mixing together salt, flour, and water. He cut the first one in the shape of a triangle and punched out a hole at the top. Later, after the dough was baked and dried, Connor painted his Christmas tree in bright colors. His mother had smiled at his handiwork, admiring it and looking pleased, before putting a red ribbon through the hole and tying it. "You get to hang this one, Connor." It became a tradition.

After moving to the city, every year Connor would bring home a new tree decoration to be added to the collection. Each year he'd search high and low for the special ornament—something unique and precious, to add to the tree. His mom would make popcorn and string it, adding the final touch to the decorations.

Connor's job was to bring down the boxes of decorations from the attic and adorn the Christmas tree from top to bottom, with the top spot reserved for the white star and angel. He was also the one to string the living room with lights.

Christmas dinner was usually early, around two in the afternoon. His mother had started inviting Mrs. Rainer after her husband died, the year she had a falling-out with her daughter, and Alana left town. Mother never pried, but she felt so bad for Mrs. Rainer, estranged from her only child.

He wondered what could have torn them apart, and how sad and lonely they must feel, especially during the holidays. Alana had been gone eight years. Life was too short to let hurt or pride stand in the way.

He felt compelled to do what he could to bring some Christmas cheer, to get them back together—if only for one day.

Chapter 16

"I'LL BE IN later." She told Ron, as he dashed inside the cabin with an armload of wood. Mary Ann needed to check her phone outside. The bars were down all the way. Later in the day, when she got back in town, she'd return calls. Connor had texted her a cute gif with a happy holiday wish. He was alone in the world. All alone except for Tom, the tabby cat, by his side. Thinking of Connor, a pang of bitterness swept over her.

Who had she been kidding?

It all made sense now. Ron's offer of partnership was the real reason Connor came back into town! Seeing him on Christmas Eve, she had gotten it all wrong. She choked back a cry.

Mary Ann pulled the scarf tighter around her neck, digging her chin inside the collar of her coat. If the brisk cold air found its way in, it would encounter her throat. She hated sore throats. She made sure to stock the special slippery elm tea in her cupboards during the winter months. But she'd forgotten to bring it to the cabin.

Ron had gone in to get the wood-burning stove going. He stood, now, in the doorway, waving her in. She went inside quickly, to warm her toes.

Ron held the door open as Mary Ann stepped across the wooden threshold. He closed the door, bringing in a swoosh of swirling snow and blast of cold wind. "Let me take your coat."

She took off her gloves first, before stuffing them in her coat pocket. "Thanks."

Mary Ann was glad she had triple-layered. Coming in from the bright snow, it took her eyes a few seconds to adjust to the gloom. The cabin was small and unassuming, furnished with just the basics. There was a wood-hewn bed pushed against a wall, a few shelves, a table, two chairs, and a wood-burning stove.

"Welcome to my humble abode," said Ron.

"I like it, and it has a rough, rugged charm in its own way," said Mary Ann, smiling as she rubbed her hands.

Water was heating on the stove. Ron rummaged in his backpack for coffee and a couple of mugs. It didn't take long before he offered Mary Ann a steaming cup of java.

She closed her eyes to take a sip. It was strong and robust, which was just the way she liked it. She wrapped her hands around the mug, capturing the warmth of it.

Ron had a funny smile pasted on his lips, as he watched her. This was the first time he'd brought a woman here. The cabin was built by his father, and it had served as a fishing and hunting camp. By the time he was old enough to come with his dad, it was only used for fishing.

His dad was a real woodsman and a survivalist. He firmly believed in being ready and prepared for the worst. He taught Ron to live in the wild; to know what to do; how to survive in the outdoors. Young Ron had imagined what it must have been like living there, back in the days when it was all wilderness; when wild animals roamed and ruled the land. Truth be told, he preferred the knowledge and modern technology of the twenty-first century. A person could have it both ways, in this world.

Chapter 17

THIS CHRISTMAS—THE first since her best friend, Connor's mom, had passed—Mrs. Rainer felt more alone than she ever had before. Her own inevitable path toward aging and dying loomed closer. She had blocked it from her mind and refused to think about it before—her own death. She was afraid. Of the unknown, of pain, of death, and of what it would feel like to die. She was frightened of what lay beyond. She feared dying alone. She couldn't stand the thought of leaving this world with no one beside her bed to say goodbye to. *Dearly departed* resonated, with an image of kneeling loved ones.

The death of Connor's mom left a void and reminded her of her own mortality. She could not escape her future. The inevitable stared in her face. It waited for her.

At Mrs. Norton's burial, Mrs. Rainer had cried again when her friend's coffin was lowered into the freshly dug ground. She had proceeded in a line of cars to the open grave. The sheriff's car led the way, with its red and blue lights flashing.

She had shuffled along with the line of mourners, each holding a single stem of a white rose. Whispered goodbyes, soft cries, and sniffles were the only accompaniment to the final act of farewell. Dottie Rainer said a silent prayer and released her flower, watching as it glided downward toward the departed. It landed gently on the coffin lid.

She took solace in knowing her friend would lie there in peace, surrounded by beautiful flowers sent by loved ones— before shovels of dirt filled the space and sunlight would no longer shine.

Mrs. Norton rested in peace, in a little piece of land marked by a headstone. This was the image Mrs. Rainer couldn't get out of her mind. Her time was coming. Her wish was for her passing to be in the spring or summer, long before the ground hardened, the trees wizened, and the birds stopped singing.

Chapter 18

AFTER MRS. NORTON'S funeral, Pastor Maller had listened to Mrs. Rainer. He didn't interrupt until she was done. He spoke soothingly, in soft tones. Mrs. Rainer confided in him about Alana, releasing the story buried inside—the ache she had carried in her heart for years. The words tumbled out and sobs came, too, interrupting and mingling with the sound of her voice until she stopped speaking altogether. She let it all out and cried, opening up the floodgates. She released the sadness welled inside, the regrets that found no relief, and the guilt that haunted her.

She cried for everyone and everything, for Alana, for herself. Mrs. Rainer sought release from the loneliness of this world. It was a world she had created, pushing away the daughter she had born and raised. Pushing her out of the safe home and into the harsh world. Forcing her out of her life.

She had kept it all inside of her: the shame, the guilt, and the cross she had to bear.

Dottie Rainer felt the gentle touch of the Pastor's hand on top of hers. His touch brought her to the present, offering comfort instead of punishment, and bringing a bit of warmth into her life.

"You're not alone."

"Please pray for me—for forgiveness," whispered Dottie, as she bowed her head.

Chapter 19

THE PLEASANT AROMA of cinnamon spice candles greeted Alana, as Connor invited her inside. The living room was decorated with sparkling lights and a tree in the middle of the room. The couch had been pushed along the wall. Tom had staked out his spot on top of it, and he was all snug and relaxed like he owned the place. His ears perked up when she arrived.

Connor took Alana's coat and hung it on the rack, smiling as he hugged her. "You're the first."

She walked to the lit Christmas tree, admiring the regular rows of lights and strings of popcorn. She smiled as she saw the decorations adorning the tree from top to bottom—the white star on top, and the angel beside it, looking down at them all.

Alana stopped by the couch to pat the cat. "How's Tom?"

"Happy to be home, like he never left," said Connor.

"Hey, remember me?" said Alana, softly. She played with

Tom, stroking the underside of his chin. As her fingers rubbed his body, his thinness became apparent. "Is he all right?" asked Alana, the alarm in her voice evident. Did the orange tabby miss Connor's mom? Did he *mourn* her passing? Or perhaps Tom missed being *here*—a country cat far from home in the city.

"He's lost weight since Mom died, after I took him with me to the city." Connor paused, the feeling of guilt washed over him.

"You take him to the vet?"

"I didn't know what else to do."

"Did it help some?"

"I want to say 'yes', but who am I kidding?" He choked back a surge of sadness. "Tom is supposed to be in my care. He's my mother's cat. But I was selfish. I was withdrawn, and barely able to take care of myself, let alone another living being."

Alana nodded but didn't interrupt.

"Tom stayed home all day when I went to work, and when I got home, I basically ignored him. I only refilled his bowl and water, sometimes not even bothering to wash his dishes." Connor's voice cracked as he continued. "Poor Tom. He must have been starved for attention and affection. But I withheld it. I didn't pet him. Because I didn't touch him, it took a while before I realized he was losing weight."

Connor sat on the couch as Alana continued to pet Tom. "I've called the vet here and got an appointment tomorrow."

"Doc Carlson?"

"He's been taking care of Tom since my mother got him.

Whatever the reason, Tom isn't his old self anymore."

"I heard about Tom showing up at your mom's doorstep one rainy day." Alana scratched behind Tom's ear and massaged his back. "Poor little guy. He was a sorry sight—soaking wet, scraggly and thin."

His heart heavy with remorse, Connor bent over to Tom's level and whispered, "I'm so sorry. Can you forgive me, fella?" *What if Tom was sick?* He had been so consumed with his own grief, he had failed at the only thing he was responsible for—the only living connection to his mother. *Oh, God, please don't let anything happen to Tom! He's innocent.* He wished tomorrow was here already, so he could see the vet right away.

The alarm on the oven sounded, summoning Connor back to the kitchen. "Come and keep me company while I finish."

Alana ruffled Tom's fur and gave him a pat. She rose, catching a delicious aroma as Connor opened the oven door. It reminded her how much she missed holiday meals at home, and pigging out on the Christmas feasts. Nothing compared to enjoying the holidays, with a good meal shared with loved ones.

"I'm making ricotta stuffed shells with spinach and tomato, roasted herb potatoes, butternut squash soup, cranberry jello, and salad," said Connor, as he poked a fork in the diced potatoes.

"Yum! What can I do?" said Alana, as she washed her hands in the sink.

"How about setting the table," said Connor, pointing

toward the cabinet where the plates were kept, and the drawer for the silverware.

"For how many?"

"Well, I'm expecting your mom, and Pastor Maller and his daughter. So that makes five of us," said Connor. He eyed the chilled jello, which was loaded with cranberries, chopped nuts, celery, and fruits—his mom's recipe. It was one of her favorites. "And we'll need glasses for the spiked eggnog and mugs for the hot cider."

Alana got to work, to ease her nervousness, busy with the task at hand. As she set the table, she couldn't help thinking of her own mother. What Dottie looked like now. Would she still be upset? How would she react, upon seeing Alana? Maybe this was a bad idea.

Connor put on the finishing touches, lighting cinnamon spice-scented candles in the dining room. Everything was perfect. Mama would be proud. He swallowed, overwhelmed with sadness. He yearned for Christmases past. He had taken so much for granted—her presence, the delicious feast she would prepare, and the family around the dinner table. Coming home for the holidays was something he never gave a second thought. He never stopped to imagine that it would end one day. It hit him hard, as reality set in. Being alone—all alone—for the first time in his life. He whispered, "Mama, I hope you're watching over us. I miss you. I love you. I wish you're here." He paused and added, "And you too, Dad."

He felt apprehensive about what the dinner would hold. There hadn't been any deliberate premeditation, before he invited Dottie and Alana. What right did he have to interfere with their family? Was it his own selfishness that made him do it? Or an unselfish desire to unite long-lost loved ones? An emptiness he sought to fill? Or was it the Christmas spirit that guided him in his actions?

He didn't mention that he had staggered the times he'd asked them to come: Alana first, then her mom, and then Pastor Maller and Eva. Was it sneaky of him to spring into action when an opportunity to reunite two lives presented itself? He'd take the blame if it didn't work out. He would find out soon.

Connor said a silent prayer, as the doorbell rang for the second time.

Chapter 20

ONE COULD SAY that Connor was a good actor. As he flung open the front door to welcome Dottie, you'd never know that anything was troubling him.

Dottie gazed around the festive room, her nose detecting delightful scents. At that moment, she felt a nostalgic Christmas cheer.

"Hello, Connor," said Dottie, as she raised her arms to hug him. Crossing the threshold, she almost expected to see his mom. She brought her homemade gingerbread cake, a favorite of Connor and his mom. But it was all different now, this year, and a wave of sadness seized her. Dottie stood in her dear friend's house, where she had been welcomed so many times. A void existed, this year. She blinked, holding back those thoughts and tears. Her friend would want her to have a happy Christmas.

A light touch on her arm brought her back to the present; to an awareness they both had; to a shared thought—a common mourning. Dottie placed her hand gently on Connor's and squeezed. She didn't need to say anything.

When the knock on the door sounded, Alana had retreated to the bathroom. She leaned on the sink, bracing with her hands, grateful for the support. She turned the faucet on and let the water run, listening to the soothing sound. The water flowed out, spattering clear droplets on the smooth surface of the sink. It seemed as if it was alive, while she had frozen, inert with anxiety.

Delaying the face-to-face meeting with her mother for one more minute, Alana turned off the faucet, finding the strength and courage to do that one inconsequential thing, when the important thing felt impossible.

Why did she come back home, after all these years? Was she crazy? When Pastor Maller told her about Connor's mom's passing, it affected her more than she expected. It didn't hit her all at once, but bit by bit. One day, as she was walking, the image of her small-town main street flashed in her mind. In the days that followed, other things triggered her memories too. She couldn't shrug them off. The way she left home, the lingering nastiness, the ill-will. She had disappeared for so long, without contacting her mother. Had she committed an unforgivable sin? Was it too late to ask for forgiveness? The thought refused to go away, showing itself, again and again, until she took action.

Alana gripped the edge of the sink again. She straightened

up and stared in the mirror. *Mirror, mirror on the wall.* If only she could ask it a question, and have it answer.

"Connor is right," said Alana. She took a deep breath. "It's time."

She turned around, opened the door of the bathroom and stepped out.

⁓❦⁓

"I need to tell you something," Connor said. "Something about today … How can I explain? I'll start at the beginning, I guess. I arrived in town. I drove through downtown, and it was more beautiful than I remembered. It was all decked out with Christmas decorations."

"I do love this time of the year. Main Street is so festive," said Dottie. The memories of happier times surfaced. "Your mom and I; we had fun shopping. One time, she was looking for a present for you. She found this stuffed bunny with a misshapen nose and a flopped ear that covered one eye—and we couldn't stop laughing."

Connor chuckled. "I know I *didn't* get that one."

"She had a knack for picking out the cutest outfits for you … and the little red dress for Alana."

"I remember," said Connor, pausing before he continued. "Yesterday I walked around downtown. I saw the coffee shop and stopped in to get a nice, hot drink." Connor smiled, adding excitement in his voice. "Guess who I ran into?"

Dottie shook her head.

"I don't understand. Who, you mean …?"

"Alana." The words escaped from Connor's lips, bursting out. "I invited her to Christmas dinner today."

Dottie gasped. "So … you invited her? *Alana?*"

"I didn't plan exactly this, but she had nowhere else to go, and it's Christmas."

"You have some explaining to do, young man," said Dottie, with a hoarse rasp.

"At the coffee shop, I didn't recognize her at first."

Dottie stared at Connor, latching on to each word.

"We talked, for a bit. Then I … well, she didn't … it just popped out. I invited her over." Connor straightened up. "Please do it for me? Let's just enjoy this meal together—on Christmas Day."

The tiny quiver of Dottie's lips betrayed her feelings, long-buried.

"Can't we just eat and be happy, today of all days?"

❦

Alana could hear the murmur of conversation.

Connor was sitting with Dottie on the couch. He caught the flickering movement as Alana approached.

Dottie followed his gaze, her eyes resting on Alana. As she stared at her long-estranged daughter, emotions wrestled within her.

No longer the gawkish teenager, Alana had become a young woman. She looked thin, but healthy. Her hair was cut short, almost like a boy. Her cotton shirt was tucked neatly in her jeans.

"I don't care what you do tomorrow," said Connor, looking between the two women. "You'll have to eventually choose if you want to work it out between the two of you. But today, while you're here …" He paused, taking a deep breath. "Please stay. You are my family, today … I invited you both here."

Connor choked, as the ache in his chest throbbed with every beat of his heart. "Do it for my mother." He stood abruptly and walked down the hallway toward his bedroom, to give them time alone. He turned his back, to hide the tears rolling down his cheeks.

Chapter 21

MARY ANN STUDIED Ron's profile as she drank her coffee. He was bent over, intent on putting more logs in the wood-burning stove, his arms stretched out. *What was she thinking, when she accepted Ron's invite?* Spending Christmas with Norma's family would've reminded Mary Ann of the emptiness in her life, still single in her thirties.

She wasn't desperate, but the ticking clock only moved in one direction. She couldn't rewind it. If someone had to use three words to describe her, it would be successful, attractive, and independent. And loving? Was this part of her description? She was capable of it. But Mary Ann was older and wiser now, not so eager to give away herself, or her heart. How would it be if she had a partner? One who loved her and supported her. Someone who was her equal. Someone who had everything going in their lives—except in the partner department.

Between work and sleep, Mary Ann didn't have much

free time. At least, that was true until she hired Norma to make sure things ran smoothly. Now, she'd run out of excuses. She thought of Connor, and the time she spent with him. That had felt … good. Then, he left town abruptly, without contacting her. Now, he was back, and he wanted to pick up where he had left things. Or had he returned for something else?

Two weeks ago, she had zero prospects. Now, she had two.

Here she was, in a cozy cabin with Ron on Christmas Day. Initially, Mary Ann had dismissed the idea of spending the day out of town. She had pictured herself curled up with a good book and a cup of tea, Isabella close by. Norma was the one who had encouraged her to go out and enjoy herself.

Her thoughts wandered. They found themselves at Connor. What was he doing? He had texted. She read his message, but with no cell coverage, she'd have to respond later. She shook her head and set her focus on the present. On Ron.

She looked out the tiny window of the log cabin. The morning flurries had ceased by the time they arrived. The air had been crisp in the freezing temperature, despite the bright sunny day. Even without the wind, it was still a harsh frozen landscape outside with a layer of fresh snow blanketing it in white.

"Mary Ann." Ron's voice broke through her thoughts.

Mary Ann took off her scarf, feeling the rising temperature warming the room. She scooted closer to the wood-burning stove.

"Hungry?"

She nodded, wondering what he had packed for lunch.

Ron reached into the insulated carrying bag. He pulled out two large containers.

Recognizing the stamped fresh market logo, Mary Ann stifled a laugh. *The man had ordered their holiday dinner takeout.* The market sold produce and cooked food to go, using organic vegetables and eggs. Their holiday meal was known to be extraordinary. She had seen the advertisements and been tempted to forgo cooking this year. She had pegged Ron as someone who didn't spend much time in the kitchen, and she was right.

He was smiling, offering the food as if she was his goddess. Okay, it wasn't quite like that, but he did have a boyish grin on his face.

"What do you have, here?" she asked him.

"A meal fit for a princess."

"Let me guess," said Mary Ann, laughing and pointing. "And you cooked it yourself."

He made a silly face, scrunching his features.

She bent over, cracking up.

Seeing her chest heaving with laughter, his lips parted, revealing his strong white teeth, adding to his charm. Ron joined her, adding his deep, hearty laugh.

Chapter 22

RON DROPPED MARY Ann off at her house around nine-thirty at night. It had been a long day. He walked around his pickup to the passenger side and opened her door.

She got out. "I've had a wonderful Christmas," said Mary Ann. She turned, glancing at her front door.

"Day's not over," prodded Ron, angling for an invite inside.

She touched his arm. "Thank you."

Ron tried to hide his disappointment, but Mary Ann caught a glimpse of it in his eyes.

"I'm tired."

"Do I get a hug?" He opened his arms wide, smiling.

She stepped up into his arms. Mary Ann was short, barely reaching up to his chest. Ron bent his head, inhaling the faint scent of her apricot honey conditioner. Her hair was soft. Stray wisps tickled his cheek. He held her, wrapping his arms around her, enveloping her small frame.

Mary Ann relaxed into the hug, feeling the warmth penetrate her coat and winter clothes. She nestled her face on the thick fabric of his jacket, finding just the spot to bury it in the slight depression of his shoulder. Was this her wish for Christmas? She had not asked for it. She had maintained the exterior of independence. Ron had chipped it, finding a tiny crack. He worked at it, as if he had taken a chisel and gently scraped the old caulk between the cracks. It had been a time-consuming process, for him.

Outside, the air was crisp. The night sky was clear, and the stars twinkled. Mary Ann closed her eyes, feeling his protective arms surround her, wrapping her like a cocoon. Like a newborn wrapped in a blanket. She could stay like this, in his arms. It was a tempting thought.

She gave him a slight push.

He released her slowly until she broke away.

She raised her head and peered into his eyes. She saw earnest adoration.

He saw a hint of promise in her eyes, of how things might be, in the future.

Mary Ann dug into her purse for her house key and walked up to the door. She turned the lock. "Good night … and Merry Christmas, Ron." She smiled at him before she stepped inside.

Isabella came up to her, meowing noisily and making her presence known, as Mary Ann closed the door.

Bending down to pick up her cat, Mary Ann took a moment to pet her before moving to the kitchen. She opened the special cat treats she got for Christmas and watched as Isabella finished them, daintily.

"Yummy?"

A lick on the chops served as an answer.

It was getting late. Mary Ann shed her clothes and jumped in the shower. Her body ached for the warm water to pulse and soothe every inch of her.

She set her mind free, letting her thoughts wander, going back over the day. It had been a rare break for her—a time for self-reflection and inspiration. A glimpse of hope, on Christmas Day. A connection with nature. It was a change of scenery she sorely needed. She was grateful that Ron had brought her to his cabin—a quiet place to relax, to be in touch with her inner self. She had been out of tune. A powerful connection was missing in her life. She had been overwhelmed with the hard work and worries involved with starting a new business, and she had shouldered a heavier burden than she had anticipated.

She had loved hearing the crunch of snow impacted by the weight of her boots, yet she almost hesitated to step on it. Disturbing the pristine white canvas felt wrong. She tried to imagine the cabin in the summertime—trees with thick, green foliage, abundant wildlife, flowers, butterflies, and bees. Being outdoors rejuvenated her, beyond anything else she could do, filling her lungs with fresh air and renewed energy.

The awesomeness of nature was breath-taking. The flowers she sold in her shop were created by it—untouched by human hand until they were cut away and harvested to adorn homes and bring joy or comfort to special occasions. Without knowing how it happened, she had gravitated to nature, to a job where she was surrounded by the most beautiful flowers, every day, in the full bloom of their beauty, some more fragrant than even the most expensive manufactured perfume. She needed to find what inspired her. She had to make sense of her future, of her past; to find the connection with the earth, and feel grounded. This was what she had almost forgotten. This was what was missing— the salve for the aches, the loneliness, and the hardships in life.

The day in the wilderness had touched Mary Ann's heart, stirring it, prodding and searching for life. It had awakened her. It had located the spirit she buried deep inside of her. This was a true gift on Christmas—unexpected and innocent. Stripped away from the commercial frenzy of the season, Mary Ann found peace, solace, and meaning. She felt like one of the animals and bare trees, who braved the harsh winter, waiting for the spring to bring new life.

Chapter 23

DOTTIE COLLAPSED IN tears, overtaken by the surprise and shock of seeing her long-lost daughter.

Alana reached out and grabbed a tissue box.

Dottie sobbed, uncontrollably, her shoulders shaking.

Staring at the stranger sitting on the couch, an image from happier times came to Dottie's mind—a little girl wearing the red dress, the one she got for Christmas one year.

"Do you remember the little red dress … the one you loved to wear?" said Dottie, her voice trembling between sobs.

Alana nodded, her eyes moist.

"I remember, when you wore it … how you twirled around and around." Dottie twisted the wet tissues in her hand. "I was afraid you'd get dizzy and fall."

"I loved the dress," said Alana. "It brings back memories. Good memories. How it used to be, when I was a little girl."

"When you were three years old."

"You loved me, then, *Mama*," said Alana. "Why can't you love me now?" She thumped her chest, crying out in anguish. "It's me. I'm still Alana." Tears gushed out.

Dottie stared at her. A vision came to her, of the last time she saw her. The words Dottie said then: harsh, cruel words, meant to cut and wound. How could she ever take it back? Did Alana still remember those three words?

As if she read her mind, Alana murmured, mouthing the very words Dottie said then.

Dottie's hopes sank, hearing them. She didn't deserve forgiveness. What she had said was unforgivable. She turned her face, as tears flowed, spilling onto her cheeks. Those words were etched in her soul. She had confessed to the Pastor—asked God for forgiveness for her sins. But she hadn't asked Alana.

"Mama!"

Flashes of the past flickered, like the fast-forward of a silent film: the day Alana was born; the first time she held Alana in her arms; the sweet smell of a newborn; the knit cap on her head, the rest of her body swaddled in a pink baby blanket. Then, the first day Alana crawled, took her first step … the first word out of her mouth.

The years flew by. More memories emerged: Alana spewing green florets and throwing her spoon across the table, when she first tasted broccoli. Alana, the toddler in the white leather shoes and a flash of red dress as she danced and twirled. The preschooler, hesitating before the door on her first day of school, reluctant to leave her mother standing outside. Then, the years afterward showed. What had gone wrong?

"Mama, talk to me."

Dottie's mouth felt dry. The upsetting memories of when her precious little girl grew up and became someone foreign to her. Someone she disapproved of. *What happened to my little girl?* Dottie had become unyielding, hardening her heart. She drove a wedge between herself and her teenaged child. They say that wounds heal, and it's true—a physical wound does. But words cut deep into the spirit; into the heart. What salve is there for these wounds?

Dottie sighed. It would not be easy to swallow her pride and admit she was wrong. It would be harder, still, to ask for forgiveness. To say those other three words: "I am sorry." The apology stuck in her throat. She shook her head and got up, moving toward the kitchen to get a glass of water.

What about Alana? Was she sorry?

Chapter 24

THE KNOCK ON the door announced the arrival of Pastor Maller and his daughter, Eva. Alana yelled to alert Connor.

Outside, it had stopped snowing. The clear, bright day brought a breath of fresh air and sunshine as Connor opened the door, mixing it with the scent of candles. He greeted Pastor Maller and Eva, warmly, and ushered them inside. He hung their coats up and carried Eva's dish of quiche into the kitchen. It was still warm from the oven. "Please, have a seat. How about some warm apple cider?"

A chorus of "Yes, please!" returned to him. Connor smiled as he got four mugs, adding one for himself. For a moment, he thought of Mary Ann. Then, he poured the cider and brought the cups out. He handed one to each person.

It had been a long time since Alana had seen the Pastor and his daughter. They engaged in an animated conversation, getting caught up. Dottie stayed quiet, but she listened intently, not missing a word. Connor interjected, once or twice, to ask Alana questions on things she had brought up. He took care not to pry into anything uncomfortable. The talk was lively, touching on highlights. At times, it was a bit sad, but they quickly moved past the hard emotions and on to the good things. Nobody brought up, or asked about, the night when Alana left.

A pleasant ding of an alarm sounded from the kitchen. "The food is ready," said Connor. "Shall we move to the dining room?" He held the chair for the Pastor, nodding to Eva to sit next to him at the table. Dottie and Alana sat across from them.

Connor brought out the dishes, before he sat at the end of the table.

"The food looks great," said Eva.

"Yeah, it's a feast," added Alana.

"Would you please pray?" said Connor, looking at the Pastor.

Pastor Maller nodded and closed his eyes. He started with the usual blessings. Then, he spoke of things more specific—of Christmas and everyone gathering together. He paused. Then, he said a heartfelt prayer—a prayer within a prayer—for Connor's mom, Mrs. Norton, and their first Christmas without her. He felt Eva's hand touch his. It was a firm grasp.

Eva was grateful for her dad. She had heard his prayers and sermons countless times. His prayers for other people— to give them hope, soothe their pain, lift them up, and bless their happiness. Prayers for babies coming into this world and those departed. Eva said a silent prayer, now, for her father. She thought of the things she wanted to say to him but had never voiced. She composed in her head a blessing for his excellent health. She had noticed his age, becoming slightly stooped as he walked. She saw his fragility, as he forsook himself for God and others.

Connor held back his tears. He wiped the corners of his eyes, grateful they were closed in prayer. He gulped and swallowed. For as long as he lived, in his thirty-eight years, he'd spent Christmas here. In the twenty years since Connor had left home, his visits had become fewer, but he made sure every year he returned for Christmas. It would never be the same again. This year, his mother's chair sat empty. This year, he honored his mom, keeping the tradition. He shared the love she gave him with the people dear to her.

Dottie squeezed her eyes shut. She missed her old friend and had felt a heavy sadness since her death. Dread and despair descended, trapping her. The only way out was through the door to her impending fate in life. Her days were numbered, marching to a clock which would one day stop.

Alana snatched a peek at her mother, opening one eye briefly. The years had not been kind to Dottie. The gray in her hair was much more pronounced than when Alana left. Her face had become more angular. The lines were more prominent. Her slight frame was thinner. But Dottie had lost more than her weight. Something had changed. How many times had Alana thought of picking up the phone and calling her mom, of coming home? Alana was ashamed. She relived the angst of the past. It was a punishment Alana dealt out to herself. The past eight years had been hard on Dottie, and she was the reason. Mrs. Norton's death had been her wake-up call, and Alana returned before it was too late. She teared up at the thought of losing her mother … and prayed for her.

Chapter 25

AFTER DINNER, EVA helped Connor with the dishes. Alana stayed at the table, sitting next to her mother. She handed her a wrapped present.

"Merry Christmas, Mom," said Alana.

Holding the neat oblong package, Dottie looked at the colorful paper and the neatly-tied ribbon. "What's this?"

"Go ahead. Open it."

Dottie slowly peeled back the taped ends, and pulled out her gift. Her eyes opened wide as she caught sight of the book title and the author. "This is *your* book?"

"Yes, it's new, just released in December," said Alana, speaking with excitement and pride.

Dottie turned it over. The back cover had a description and a photo of Alana. "This is your story ... *The Runaway*."

Alana nodded. "Like the photo?"

"It's casual, but it looks professional."

"Look inside," said Alana, flipping the pages to her

inscription. "I signed the book."

"I see, and you dated it December twenty-fifth," said Dottie.

"One more thing. Turn the page."

Tears welled up in Dottie's eyes when she saw Alana had dedicated the book to her mother and father.

Alana reached over and grabbed a clean napkin on the table. "Here, use this."

"Thank you."

"Mama, what happened was an accident."

"Which part? You never meant to be caught?" said Dottie, talking between sniffles.

"I never meant for any of it."

"That night …"

"I waited until everyone was asleep before I got up."

"You thought everyone was sleeping."

"I snuck in the kitchen; to the secret place where I knew you kept it."

"Why?"

"I thought I had enough money for Christmas, but something unexpected threw the best-laid plans off."

"So, you stole money."

"Yes, but it wasn't for me, and I planned to replace it before you found out."

"Your dad …"

"I jumped when he came up behind me. He'd gotten up to get a drink of water in the kitchen."

"Caught you in the act."

Alana looked down, her cheeks aflame.

"He was furious, livid with anger … like I've never seen him," said Alana. "He grabbed me. I was still holding on to the money. I wouldn't let go." She wet her lips. "We struggled."

"I woke up to the noise," said Dottie. "I saw him falling to the floor, gripping his chest." She paused. Reliving the moment was difficult. "I rushed to him and called 911."

Alana said nothing. She'd give anything to relive that moment; to give back her father's life. All she could remember was her mother's chilling words, spat out in the heat of the moment, without thinking. Those three accusatory words: "You're killing him."

Chapter 26

December 26

CONNOR PULLED INTO the parking lot of Doc Carlson's office. It was housed in a nondescript building. A solitary, faded sign—which said "Veterinary Care"—hung over the doorway. It was quiet. Low bushes lined the somber gray cement of the walkway. Behind curtains, a soft glow lit up the building.

It was early morning, a few minutes before eight, on the day after Christmas. The lot was empty, except for a dusty pickup, which probably belonged to the vet. Connor had called the Doc and left a message. In the city, he wouldn't have expected to get an appointment over the holidays. Good old Doc Carlson had called him right back and gave him the first available slot. In this small town, the good Doc put his patients first.

During the journey, Tom had been curled up in the pet carrier. He was alert and awake, now. He knew something was going on. And he was pissed. He didn't like to be cramped and locked up in a tiny cell. *Imprisoned like a criminal!* He'd have none of it. His funk had gone from bad to foul. The mood had begun when he was awakened early that morning, at the most inopportune moment—just as he dreamed of catching the mouse. The tip of its tail was flickering in front of Tom's whiskers. His prey was inches from his grasp …

"Hey, guy, yes you," said Connor, adding as much charm as he could muster, when talking to his cat.

Tom didn't even blink an eye.

He bent, putting his face closer to the wire door of the carrier. "I know you're not going to like this." Connor stifled a laugh—no point in rubbing it in.

Connor stopped his humiliating baby talk. By golly, Tom was a full-grown cat! He remembered how Tom was: how he stood and strutted in all his glory. *A ferocious mice hunter!*

"It's okay, fella. I'm going to get you all checked out, ready for the new year," said Connor.

Connor turned the car key, cutting off the engine. He reached for Tom's carrier. "Let's go get this over with." *For you and me both*, he wanted to add.

The bell chimed, when Connor opened the door. The waiting room hadn't changed much from the last time he was here, with his mom. Doc Carlson was a no-frills kind of guy and didn't waste money on interior decoration. The Doc never married. To put it another way, he was married to his work. The loves of his life were his animal patients. In his younger days, he used to do house calls. As the years rolled on, he established an office and did less traveling.

"Doc Carlson?" said Connor, nodding to the man in a white coat standing behind the counter. He looked older, the patches of white hair having wholly taken over. His lips seemed thinner and sterner. His head was tilted forward a bit, his shoulders slightly rounded. But the blue eyes that stared back at Connor were bright and sharp, like the mind behind them.

"You're Mabel Norton's boy," said the Doc, as he greeted him.

Connor extended his free hand in greeting. "Yes, sir. Connor Norton." He turned the carrier a bit, so the front door would face the vet. "And this is my mama's cat, Tom."

The Doc chuckled. "I sure remember Tom."

Connor gave him his full attention.

"That day, he was a sorry sight, all wet and scrawny-looking, but your mama poured all her love on him, and nursed him back to health." He paused, eyes on the cat. "You'd hardly recognize Tom, after he was cleaned up and recovered. He was gorgeous—all orange stripes, with round, green eyes and long whiskers."

"He sure is a handsome fellow," said Connor. "He was all I had, after my mother passed. I took him back to the city with me."

"Let's take a look at him," said Doc Carlson, leading the way to the examination room down the hall.

Connor put the carrier on the counter in the middle of the room. He opened the hatch. Tom needed no coaxing to come out, extending his legs to stand on firm ground.

"I'm worried about him. He's losing weight."

"How long has this been going on?"

"I'm not sure," said Connor, wracked with guilt over his neglectful behavior.

"You've had him for a few months?"

"About four months."

"Take him to see a vet in the city?"

Connor nodded and reached in his coat pocket. "I have this." He retrieved a few pages of folded papers and handed them to the vet. "They ran some tests. Here are the lab results of blood samples they took."

Doc Carlson glanced at the numbers, dated mid-December. The city vet had done extensive testing, ruling out kidney disease or renal failure, liver disease, hyperthyroidism from excessive amounts of thyroid hormone, diabetes, tumors, digestive disorders, and other conditions. There were no abnormal results. The city vet even did X-rays.

"His kidney and thyroids—"

"Checked out fine. He looks to be in good health."

Connor let out a sigh of relief on hearing the last part: 'in good health'. "But he's losing weight."

Doc Carlson weighed Tom and gave him a physical. "Seven-and-a-half pounds."

Connor tensed, his heart rate sped up.

"Let's try this." He wrote the brand name of a cat food on a piece of paper and handed it to Connor. "Adjust his diet gradually. Be sure the cat food is on a clean plate, especially wet food. Do you give him fresh water daily, in a clean water bowl?"

"I've been too busy at work … I've been forgetting to clean his bowls or change the water." Connor fidgeted, uncomfortable about admitting to his role in Tom's condition.

Doc Carlson's eyes pierced through Connor's flimsy excuse. Mabel would not have neglected her cat, and Tom had been Mabel's constant companion until she died. Could the shock of losing her have affected Tom?

"Have you noticed any changes in Tom, after Mabel died?"

"He's lost interest in food," said Connor. "And he seemed to have less energy and he's sleeping more."

"You took him to the city. What kind of place did you have?"

"I had a two-bedroom condo. It wasn't a high-rise."

"Did you have a yard?"

Connor shook his head. "Not much of one. Space was at a premium, and the designers chose to optimize the square footage of the living area."

"So, Tom stayed indoors while you went to work?" said Doc Carlson.

"Yes."

"How long did you leave him?"

"I leave for work early and get home by dark most days. It would be about ten to twelve hours."

"Those are long hours."

"I'm used to them," said Connor. He attempted a joke, adding, "It's the price you pay for an office with a window." Above him, only the top executives got the corner offices with windows on two sides.

"What did Tom do, while you were gone?"

Connor looked up, his mind switching back to the cat. Honestly, he didn't know. "He had the whole condo to himself. He was alone."

Doc Carlson didn't have the fancy equipment of the city vets. But he was a skilled diagnostician. His years of experience and his talent earned him the respect of many owners.

"Did you know animals can grieve?" asked Doc Carlson.

Connor stared at the older man, trying to translate this. He hadn't thought of Tom as grieving.

"You mean Tom could be in mourning?"

"From what you've described of Tom's behavior, and the changes he's experienced, I'd have to say 'yes'."

"From losing my mom?"

"Your mom was his constant companion. It was just the two of them, living in the house." Doc Carlson spoke firmly, and steadily. "Not only that, the change in environment when you moved Tom from the small town to the city—from your mom's house to the condo." He paused. "And being alone in a strange environment all day."

Connor digested all this information—all these changes must have affected Tom. *Poor fella.* "I must admit I failed with Tom. I was absorbed in my own world … my grief."

"Tom would have sensed it too—*your* grief."

"Poor Tom." Connor just wanted to beg for his forgiveness and hide. *How could he have done this?* Tom was the only living thing he had left in the world, after his mom died. The cat was her companion to the end.

"Mabel loved this orange boy, dearly," said Doc Carlson. "If it wasn't for Tom, she may not have lived that long."

Doc Carlson's brow furrowed. He opened his mouth to give Connor a piece of his mind, but the remorse on Connor's face stopped him.

"Let's just keep a close eye on Tom. Will you be staying a bit?"

"I've quit my job in the city."

"You'll be here?"

"At least until I figure out what to do with my life."

"There are a few things you can do to help him."

Connor nodded, eagerly, hoping for a chance to do something before it was too late. "Anything."

"Spend more time with Tom. Since you've quit your job, you're not going to leave him alone all day. Touch can be healing, for both of you."

"I can do that."

"Get yourself a cat comb or brush. Pet Tom, brush him, talk and sing to him. Do whatever you can do, to connect."

"I'm afraid singing is out of the question," said Connor.

"Play some music. Pick something your mother liked. Ease him back. Let him go outside."

Connor laughed, pointing his finger. "You should see Tom in action outdoors. He loves to chase butterflies. And he gets in plenty of trouble going after his favorite rodents."

Doc smiled. "Your mom was fond of retelling Tom's feats: how he'd carry his prized mouse in his mouth and laid it on her front door mat."

"But she never scolded him."

"No, she made a big fuss over Tom, and thanked him for his gift by giving him special treats."

Connor glanced at Tom—the smart, beautiful, healthy and muscular cat he was. And now he's just lying there, muscles limp and out of practice. He made a promise to Tom. *We'll have to change things.*

"Bring Tom back in a couple of weeks. We'll see how he's doing," said Doc Carlson.

Connor stopped by the store on his way home, to pick up the new cat food, bowl, and a plate for Tom, along with a comb and a brush. Visual reminders of change. Those were easy gifts: the ones money could buy. What Connor needed to do was to give Tom the gift of time and his love. Gifts from the heart. It was time Connor honored his mother and took proper care of the cat she loved so much.

Chapter 27

AFTER SEEING DOC Carlson, Connor stopped by in town to see Mr. Monroe, the attorney. Going up the steps, he could see a little sign posted on the door. The business was closed for the holidays, until January second. Connor wasn't surprised. He would call and make an appointment to be sure his parents' affairs were settled.

He continued the short walk to the flower shop. Mary Ann had texted him back, a nice thanks and well wishes. He'd figured she'd have holiday plans, and he hadn't expected her to drop everything and spend Christmas with him, when he appeared out of nowhere on Christmas Eve. Connor was curious about who she had spent her day with. The expectations he had of her were all his own making; in his own mind. He hadn't taken any action or kept in touch, for four months. What right did he have to expect anything from her? It was a stretch, but he had a lively imagination. Mary Ann had been the bright spot in his life, after his mother passed. He had kept her in mind. Connor had no right to expect anything from her. Was he a cold-hearted, selfish man? Was he ready for a partner? Connor couldn't even take care of a cat.

He stopped, steps away from her flower shop. Then, he slowly turned around and walked away.

Chapter 28

MARY ANN CARRIED the chalkboard, setting it down behind the counter. It was Norma's idea. It was now a ritual to write on the chalkboard in the morning, and it got her creative juices flowing. She opened her tray of colorful chalks and got started. The flowers changed weekly, and it was seasonal. She drew the flowers, wrote out the name and added a short factoid, about the plant she'd drawn.

If there was a sale or a promotion on, or a holiday around the corner, she'd add the details of that too. Now, she erased the 'Merry Christmas' and replaced it with 'Happy Holidays.' Soon, it would be changed to a New Year greeting.

She thought about the day before, in the cabin with Ron, and the hug they had shared afterward. She'd almost hung mistletoe on her porch but didn't get it done in time. It would have assured a kiss! She wondered what a kiss with Ron would have been like. She had said 'yes', when Ron invited her to his cabin. She was ready for a change in scenery, and it felt good to get away. Ron had called, and let her know he had a good time. She smiled.

"Someone had a nice Christmas," said Norma. She walked in wearing a new coat, carrying her purse in one hand.

Mary Ann blushed.

"C'mon, out with all the juicy details."

"I'd rather admire your new coat."

Norma stopped in front of Mary Ann and unbuttoned it. "Feel how soft it is."

"It suits you," said Mary Ann. Her hand caressed the soft fabric. *It must be a new blend,* she thought. It wasn't scratchy and rough, like wool. "And camel tan is your favorite color. So, how did Stan know exactly what you wanted?"

"I don't pussyfoot around. Not when it comes to what I want." Norma took off her gloves, pulling one finger at a time. She started with the thumb and worked her way down. "I tell him."

Mary Ann watched Norma fold her gloves and stuff them in her pocket.

Norma cleared her throat. "And if that doesn't get the message across, I cut out the picture in the catalog, or print it off the internet, and hand it to Stan."

"That's clear as mud," said Mary Ann. She couldn't resist a little tease.

"Back to where we were. You changed the subject," said Norma. Nothing much got by her. Not when it came to the customers. Not when it came to Mary Ann. "So, you had a good time with Ron?"

"I ... I warmed up to it—the cabin, him, well ... everything."

"You see what you would have missed by not going?"

Mary Ann laughed, then leaned back to admire her handiwork on the chalkboard. "What do you think?"

Norma nodded her approval. "I like it."

"I think I'll leave this up until New Year's Eve," said Mary Ann. "Four more days, then we start over for a new year."

"You got plans?"

"I'll probably be snug in bed." *Or I'll be partying with Ron*, Mary Ann thought.

"Not big on watching fireworks?"

"Maybe I'll watch it on TV, if I'm up. You guys have a celebration?"

"Not a big one. We'll have dinner with the kids."

"Well, good," said Mary Ann. Satisfied with her finished artwork, she set the chalkboard easel display on the sidewalk.

Chapter 29

December 31

CONNOR WOKE UP early on New Year's Eve. He spent a quiet holiday in his mother's home, aside from seeing Mrs. Rainer again when she came by. He had been touched by her kindness; her visit to see how he and Tom were doing.

He had actually considered inviting her to his mom's house, for a New Year's Eve brunch. But she beat him to it. Dottie Rainer had sounded chipper when she called, which had made him feel a bit sad, if he was completely honest. Connor was fighting off a bout of doldrums after Christmas. When Mrs. Rainer extended the invitation, he quickly accepted. It might cheer him up.

He made two dishes to bring: an asparagus mushroom casserole he'd converted from his mom's old recipe, and his own signature salad. Growing up in Rocky Flats, Connor had even foraged for wild mushrooms when they were seasonal, and made this substitution in her recipe. Now, he still enjoyed being creative and experimenting with food.

Connor had been thinking about food a lot lately. He was even considering getting a part-time job at the fresh market, cooking. He had thought long and hard about Ron's offer to be partners at his hardware store. Connor had called him back to thank him for his generosity, but to say he couldn't accept. He apologized for taking so long to respond. It wasn't a decision Connor made lightly. In the end, he went by his inner voice. He knew his heart wasn't in it.

At two o'clock, he walked next door to Dottie's, taking Tom with him. Her place had become drab and neglected, after her husband died and Alana left. When Connor knocked on the door, Dottie flung it open, immediately.

"Well, do come in," said Dottie. She was acting like an excited hostess.

"Oh, Wow!" Connor's face registered surprise upon seeing the pleasing freshly-painted walls.

Before he could set his food down, Alana appeared. "I'll take it to the kitchen."

"You're here!"

"I've been busy working," said Alana, waving her arms across the living room. "Like my paint job?"

"It looks great," said Connor. "You've done wonders for this place." He hadn't seen Alana and had been wondering if she'd left town again. So, this was what had kept her busy.

Before long, Pastor Maller and Eva arrived, too. It was like one happy family again.

During dinner, Dottie told them what happened after she went home on Christmas. She had read Alana's book and cried, long and hard, finally coming to terms with the night Alana left. She had asked her daughter for forgiveness.

One question kept bugging Connor. He turned to Alana. "The night it happened, why did you take the money?"

"I needed it, to help out a friend."

"Couldn't you have just asked your mother?"

Alana shook her head. "No, I promised I wouldn't tell."

"So, you thought you had to steal the money?"

"Yes. I knew it was wrong, but my friend counted on me. She was in trouble and couldn't tell her parents."

"We've forgiven each other," said Dottie. "Alana came home. It's all that matters."

Alana smiled. "I love you, Mom." She turned and gave her mom a hug. She planted a tender kiss on Dottie's cheek, before releasing her.

Dottie looked up at her tall, lovely daughter; the spark back in her eyes. "I love you, Alana."

"I'm home, Mama."

Chapter 30

December 31

HE USED TO love New Year's. After the hustle and bustle of the holidays, it meant one more day of relaxing and having fun. One more day before he went back to work. But it had all changed, this year. He cut the chains that were pulling him back. The coveted office with the window he'd finally reached seemed of little consequence, now. The many years he'd invested in achieving this goal left a taste of bitterness.

Connor looked forward, now. For the first time in many years, he felt a stir of anticipation; of a new adventure—the bloom of new life.

Even Tom had changed. Connor watched the cat's chest rise and fall, with each breath. Connor let him sleep, not disturbing him. Since coming back to his childhood home, Tom had slowly slipped into his old habits, finding his favorite nooks and crannies. He was taking possession of the place, again, like it was his home—which it was. He jumped up on the couch, the bed, or wherever he felt like plopping down. He even explored the snow.

Connor propped up a makeshift window seat in the living room, so Tom could look out the window to his heart's content. It took little to make him happy. Connor could count the ways on his fingers.

He suspected the move from the city had done wonders for Tom. He enjoyed watching him revert to his old self again. Wise Doc Carlson had been right. The little spark had not been extinguished.

Tom had come home. So had Connor.

Chapter 31

Around Midnight, December 31

MARY ANN LED Ron outside her place, a few minutes before the stroke of midnight. "I want to see the stars tonight." Faint popping sounded in the distance.

Ron enjoyed spending time with Mary Ann. Ever since the trip to his cabin on Christmas, they'd been almost inseparable. He liked the things they had in common, her understated sense of humor, and her strengths. Her adventurous side, as well as her reserved side. He was patient, earning her trust bit by bit. As she became more open, and exposed her vulnerabilities, he felt protective. He couldn't deny the strong attraction and a growing fondness—something special he'd never felt before, for any other person.

They stood together under the clear night sky. Side by side. "It's beautiful," said Ron. He wrapped his arm around her shoulder, pulling her closer.

She curled her arm, reaching behind his back and around his waist, and whispered his name.

The moon was visible. The stars twinkled across the vast expanse of space, as far as the eye could see. It was breathtaking. A natural canvas that no human painter could ever recreate.

As midnight approached, Ron turned to face Mary Ann. His fingertips affectionately caressed her cheek. She tilted her face. They stared into each other's eyes; deep into each other's souls.

At the stroke of midnight, their lips met for the first time.

Author's note

I hope you've enjoyed this sequel to *Flowers in December*.

Thank you for reading!

Acknowledgments

Thanks to my family and friends and Thiago Ding for your love and support, editors and Polgarus Studio and everyone who's been a part of this book—in one way or another.